Fire and Ice

By

Diana Bellerose

Copyright © 2011 by Diana Bellerose

ISBN 978-0-7414-7035-5

Printed in the United States of America

This is a work of fiction. Names, characters, places, and incidents either are the product of the author's imagination or are used fictitiously. Any resemblance to actual events or locales or persons, living or dead, is entirely coincidental.

Published February 2013

INFINITY PUBLISHING
1094 New DeHaven Street, Suite 100
West Conshohocken, PA 19428-2713
Toll-free (877) BUY BOOK
Local Phone (610) 941-9999
Fax (610) 941-9959
Info@buybooksontheweb.com
www.buybooksontheweb.com

ACKNOWLEDGEMENTS

I am extremely grateful to so many people without whom the publication of my book would not have been possible. For their support and constant encouragement, I want to thank my family first, my friends: Ylva Karlsson, Vicki Curran, Jackie Ross and Valli Kemp. Special thank you to Elle Febbo Author and Advocate, who I am so lucky to know for her constant collaboration in the process of editing and publishing my book. I want to thank you also the designer of my book cover Kenny Covington for his generosity and collaboration.

Best wishes to
Pete Seaman from

Diana Bellerose

Seattle WA
5/7/2016

TABLE OF CONTENTS

Chapter I 1

Chapter II 11

Chapter III 22

Chapter IV 25

Chapter V 29

Chapter VI 34

Chapter VII 37

Chapter VIII 42

Chapter IX 52

Chapter X 60

Chapter XI 64

Chapter XII 66

Fire and Ice

I

Nancy was sitting at home trying to sort out her life. Trying to figure out what had gone wrong and what could be done to fix it. The weather was windy and rainy. Summer was almost over. There was something to look forward to, her trip to Hawaii. She was hoping to clear her head there and start finding some solutions. She was sitting at the kitchen table having a cup of freshly brewed coffee. The sun was peeking through the window. The room was full of light. Nancy's expression was one of pain and worry. There were so many obstacles in her life, each taking a toll on her. The troubles she was having were with her husband and the family's financial situation. It was hard to cope anymore despite the fact that she considered herself a very strong person. Having no one around to support her made her even more vulnerable. Her husband was unsupportive and violent and was the worst part of her life. She had endured his abuse for twenty years. The load was getting too heavy, and she was not young enough anymore to be able to ignore certain things.

Though she lived in America, she had been born and raised in Poland, Europe. Nancy was a beautiful woman with blue eyes and light brown hair. Her parents had divorced when she was thirteen years old, after her mother had suffered being abused for years by her father. The problems she had as a child did not help. Nancy was thirty-nine years old, and her whole life was centered on her family. She was a devoted wife and mother who never found time to do anything about the problems in her own life. She did not feel secure in her relationship and did not know what the future held for her. Her husband, with whom she owned a business, was giving up on everything they had worked hard for because they owed so much money to the banks. Times were hard. It was the Great Recession, and the business was not making enough to cover all of the expenses.

Nancy and her husband had been high school sweethearts. They met when she was in high school at a mutual friend's party. It was love of first sight, and they had been together since then. His parents never liked her and never gave them their approval. This had taken a toll on their marriage, and they were never left alone.

Her husband's name was Tom. He was a tall, handsome, dark-haired man with piercing brown eyes. Tom was an only child. His parents had met in their late thirties. Tom's father was a divorced dad with a daughter, and his mother was a single woman. Nancy and Tom had a beautiful, nineteen-year-old daughter named Jen. Jen had never known her grandparents. They lived so far away. Nancy and Tom had moved to the United States when Jen was only a baby. The only grandparent she knew was Nancy's father, who had married for a second time and had a daughter. His wife never wanted Nancy's family around. She wanted to keep everything for herself and her daughter, and Nancy's dad followed her strict orders. He saw his only granddaughter once a year, and sometimes only once every two years.

Nancy's mother, Rose, had been living with her second husband for twenty-five years. Nancy had never liked him. Her mother had changed a lot when she met that man. She was no longer this gentle, loving mother anymore. Her mother's new husband, Bob, wanted Nancy out of the house, which had been given to her mother because Nancy was under her care. Nancy was often thrown out onto the street because of arguments with this new man in her mother's life. Nancy had felt pressured to marry Tom early to escape the torture of living with her mother and her mother's new husband.

Things changed drastically when Nancy and her husband decided to go back and visit their parents in Europe. Her mother decided to have a will drawn up, so she could leave part of her estate to Nancy. The house had already been divided among her mother, her younger brother, and Bob, her mother's husband. Nancy was to inherit the part that belonged to her mother after her death. When her mother's husband found out, he became angry. He had been hoping to get Nancy's mother's part for himself. So, after Nancy and her family came back home, Bob started beating Nancy's mother every day. Rose was a dark-haired, petite woman. The house she was living in was a two-story home with a beautiful mountain view. Everything was brand new inside and out. There were gardens with flowers on every side of the house. Bob and Rose were doing a lot of gardening. Bob was so proud of the way he was maintaining the property. He could not accept the idea of Nancy having a part of the home she had once left because of him.

Nancy was devastated and did not know what to do. Her brother was visiting at the time, and he had to return to Europe early to see what could be done to stop this abuse. His name was John, and he was a tall, twenty-five-year-old man with light hair and green eyes. He was a very well-mannered young person, and it was hard for him to cope with his raging stepfather. Bob also started attacking John on a daily basis. John was very upset about it, and one day he told Rose, "Mother, I can't take this any longer, so I am on my way to find a place of my own. Please understand me and don't be angry with me. I have my life to live as well. Having a crazy person around the house and being attacked is not something I can put up with." John was forced to rent an apartment to escape all of the craziness. He was not the type of man who would jump into a fight, so he left.

Nancy's mother was left to endure this torture alone. There was no way to throw Bob out, because he had his share of the house. It was hard on Nancy's family, but there was not much they could do to help. Bob would scream at Nancy, "You made the biggest mistake ever by giving your part to her. What you were thinking? Now I must share everything with her family." Bob believed that Rose should have asked him first before she decided to leave her share of the house to Nancy. "I don't like when I am not asked for my approval. That is why you are going to put up with my treatment. If you don't like it, you know what you can do." Nancy's mother was devastated because she never expected Bob to show so much anger towards her. He had always been very nice and loving towards her. Now, with his being physical towards her, it was sad situation.

Tom's mother, Jen, died a month after their return to America, and their lives were in shambles. Tom had to go back for her funeral. It was not the best time, but he again had to spend money they did not have to go back, money that was so pivotal at that moment. Money was a big issue, and the business was getting worse because of the recession. Everything was going wrong. The value of their house started to decline, and their debt was building up like a mountain. Nancy's mother, Rose, was calling in the middle of the night complaining about the abuse she was receiving from her husband. Nobody was interested in helping her. In some countries, the police consider domestic violence a family matter and do not interfere until somebody gets beaten to death. Then they just come and gather the bodies. Even if the police decide to come to the home, they have to ask permission from both parties before entering. If the man does not want to let them in, they just leave and do not do anything. As a result, so many women end up dead. It sounds harsh, but this is how it is. Tom was getting very upset and annoyed by the late night calls from Nancy's mother.

"Why is your mother calling so late?" he asked Nancy one night. "Why doesn't she try to save you some trouble and not tell you what's going on?"

"This is my mother, Tom," Nancy answered him, "and I am the only one she can talk to!"

Tom continued, "Tell her to call in the morning. I have to work and I need my sleep. I'm sure she can wait until tomorrow. What does she want you to do when you're on the other side of the globe?"

Nancy had to deal with so many problems. On one side were her mother and her husband, and on the other Tom and his drinking. Tom was an alcoholic, and he was drunk every night. When he was drunk, he would get violent and wait for a small thing to start yelling and screaming about like he was in agony. It was hard to keep him under control. He would break things around the house. When Jen was home, she was usually the one who could get some control over him. One night he was so drunk that he started to break dishes he had taken from the kitchen cabinets.

"Now I am going to destroy this house which is giving me so much trouble. Let me see what you two are going to do about it. Maybe call the police and tell them what? It is my home, and I can do whatever I want, even set it on fire." It was so sad for Nancy and Jen to see the gorgeous home being destroyed in front of their eyes. The house was a very nice contemporary home with high ceilings and wooden floors. Nancy was a great housekeeper, and her home was very important to her. She always had a vase with fresh flowers on her living room table. Her favorite scent was vanilla, so the whole house had this scent. Everything looked great. The only problem was Tom's bad habits and the problems they had had for a long time because of them. This had been Nancy and Jen's life for years. Before the death of Tom's mother, things had been even worse. Tom's mother was always planting her hate towards Nancy into Tom's head. Every time he called her, he would get off the phone and act strange, like he was ready to go into a battle. At these times, Tom would get drunk and attack Nancy by starting arguments over nothing. His favorite time was in the evening when everybody was at the kitchen table having a nicely prepared dinner.

Nancy was not only a great housekeeper, she was a wonderful cook. Her meals were always delicious. Everything that she did was done with love and care. Tom would start arguing at dinner without showing any remorse towards Nancy or Jen. One night he told Nancy,"I don't like the way you cooked this soup," he would say. You should have used less water. It doesn't taste right. How many times do I have to repeat myself? You never listen. What do you want me to do now, eat something that tastes like water?"

Poor Nancy and Jen, they had to eat and tolerate his abusive language. Every time Nancy tried to calm down the situation, it not only did not do any good, but it did the opposite. Situations like this were an ongoing problem in the house. Dinner time was a nightmare after Tom had had one too many drinks. He had so much negative energy in his heart and soul.

His mother took her grudge toward Nancy to her grave. She could not accept Nancy. She thought Nancy was not the right one for her son. She had never loved or accepted Jen either, because she had a theory: "Like mother, like daughter." Tom's mother also thought Nancy was like her mother, who was, in her opinion, the worst human being. Why? Because when Tom's mother would call Rose to tell her that her daughter was not a good match for her son, Rose was not supportive of the opinion. She would constantly call Rose at work and give her the usual lecture: "I think that it is just about time for you to understand that my son is not for sale, and your daughter should back off and stop calling him. I promise you that if you do not take drastic measures now, I will, and you are not going to like it. If you love your daughter, and do not want her to get into a family which does not want her, now is the time to act. I am warning you, and I am not going to change the way I feel. It is up to you as a mother to stand up and save her and yourself a lot of trouble."

Rose would reply, "I don't think that you are taking seriously what is going on between those children. I don't want to argue with you, and I think that we should postpone this conversation till the right time comes. Right now, I am at work, and I would appreciate it if you would not call me so often here. Don't call me when I'm at work unless it is an urgent matter and cannot wait."

Jen would answer, "Don't tell me that I did not warn you. I am telling you good-bye now, and I'll talk to you again."

Rose would say, "Thank you for the warning. I appreciated it and good-bye."

Nancy's mother was an open-minded woman who did not see the young couple as being even close to marriage when they were dating. In her eyes, they were two kids in love and nothing more. On the contrary, Tom's mother saw them as married couple already and saw Nancy as the worst choice for her son. She would tell Tom, "Don't you see that this girl is not even close to our status in society? She comes from a troubled family, and your father and I don't want you to have anything more than a little romance with her. We don't want her to be part of our family. So please, Son, do not makes us worry. I know she is a beautiful girl right now, but sooner or later, this will go away and you will end up with nothing to be attracted to. This girl has no potential, and she has never been able to go to college for a better education. Look at her mother and father; they are simple and troubled people. She will not ever be anything more than they are."

To defend himself, Tom would tell his mother, "Don't worry, Mother, I know what I'm doing. You don't have anything to worry about for now. We're too young for marriage, and we have plenty of time before we even consider something like that. I love her very much, and we're experiencing falling in love for the first time, like so many people our age. I really don't think that you should even consider marriage as an issue at this time in our relationship. The best thing for you to do is to leave everything to me and trust me."

Jen was the kind of person who would not listen to anybody. She always had her mind made up about everything in life. The only thing that mattered to her was her way of seeing things. That is why she never left Tom and Nancy or Nancy's mother alone. She was continually calling and even visiting Nancy's home. She was constantly in their lives, causing drama when they were teenagers having fun and not even knowing yet if they were going to get married someday. Tom's mother was bent on poisoning their romance as much as she could, because she could not accept that her opinion did not matter and that nobody listened to what she had to say. It was her way or no way. She was a very stubborn and ambitious person who had never had a friend because of it. People would stay away from her because they knew she was trouble.

Tom's family had a couple of close friends who used to get together with them to eat and drink. At Tom's house, eating and drinking was the most important part of life. His house was huge and was filled with nice furniture. There were shelves with so many souvenirs on them. It was cozy and clean, and everything was in its place. Tom's mother was a great housekeeper, and her cooking was amazing. Their favorite dish was meatballs with a specially prepared sauce. Tom's father was extremely picky when it came to food, so Jen was the best match for him. Money was never an issue. When his parents got married, they moved into his father's aunt's house. His aunt's husband had been a physician and had made a good living. Unfortunately, he had died very young, and his widow had inherited the house. The house was very well maintained, with rose bushes on both sides of the path which led to the front door. There were fruit trees and a lot of flowers. It looked like a sanctuary. Tom's great aunt was a very spoiled housewife, and her husband's death was hard on her. So she decided to adopt Tom's father, along with his twelve-year-old daughter from his first marriage. She had never been able to have children, but her sister had five children. In order to help him to have a good future, Tom's grandmother gave Tom's father to her.

When Tom's mother moved into the house, she inherited a daughter, and soon after that gave birth to Tom. Tom's dad made good money, and his family never had any money problems. Having a home and not paying rent was an additional reason for not worrying about money. His mother was always telling people about how good her life was and the places she had visited. Their life had always been a privileged one. She had even had the opportunity to travel to Paris and other great cities in Europe, which was something unthinkable for most people at the time, because they had no way to afford it.

Sam and Nancy named their daughter after Tom's mother. This was one of Tom's mother's wishes. It was a tradition in their country to name one's child after one of the mothers's or father's parents. Nancy was not happy, but she had no choice or right to choose. She was forced to live with Tom's parents because this was Tom's mother's orders when they got married.

Jen would tell Tom, "You two are going to live with us because I want to make sure that my son is well taken care of. A young housewife cannot prepare very good meals. She has to learn from her mother-in-law before she will be ready to take care of her son. I am an excellent wife and cook, so it is good for her to live with us in the beginning."

Tom was a Mommy's boy and had no right to an opinion. The ruling lady never gave him a chance to tell her how he felt. Living with his parents never gave him a chance to adjust to his life as a married man and to feel like the man of the house. Nancy was never given the right to feel like a wife or the option of choosing what was right for her. They were just two children sleeping in the same bed every night and not having the right to express how they felt or to do what they liked in this arrangement. The only thing that mattered was that Tom's mother was happy and that whatever she said and did was unconditionally accepted.

Nancy's mother minded her own business and never forced her opinion on the young family. She would help them with what she had and with what she could do for them. Nancy's mother lived very close by, and they visited Nancy's home often. Nancy had to quit her job because Tom's father had never approved of it. The problem was that her job involved nightshifts. He told Nancy and Tom, "I do not want my daughter-in-law to go to work when I am going to sleep. There is no way for me to agree on something like this." Since money was never an issue, he never felt that Nancy's money would matter. Nancy spent a lot of time at her house because she loved to be around her mother and brother. It was very convenient for her because her mother lived very close by. She did not have need of any transportation. This got on Tom's mother's nerves.

Jen was always secretly complaining to Tom about Nancy spending a lot of time at her house instead of staying home and adjusting to her married life. She would tell him, "I feel that my daughter-in-law should stop spending so much time at her house with her family. She has a new home now, and she should start to clean her room more often and try to make friends with the neighborhood women. What was the point of getting married if she is going to go and spend so much time at her old house? I think, Son, that you should step in and, as her husband, try to tell her that."

This was just one of her ways of controlling Tom and Nancy and creating tension between them. Every time there was trouble, she was the mastermind. This way, she made herself happy and fed their conflict. She was an evil person whose main intention was to make people around her miserable when things were not going her way. Nancy was her captive target, and she fully enjoyed it when they argued because of her. Her constant presence in the young married couple's life took a toll on them. Things became even worse because Nancy was getting sick of her mother-in-law's rules. Nancy knew that all of her troubles were caused by her mother-in-law, but she was not able to defend herself because Tom was a "good son" who was convinced that his mother always said and did things with the best intentions.

Nancy would try to tell Tom, "Don't you see that your mother is always creating problems for us? She does that to us because she wants to get even with me. Our being married was the last thing she wanted, and now she enjoys every argument we have! I think that we are old enough to solve our problems, and we don't need her opinion every time we have a problem. Can you please tell her that?"

Tom would answer her, "I think that my mother is right about some things, and I want her opinion. She is right as well when she tells me that you should stop spending so much time with your mother and try to stay here more. I want my mother to be in our life. She knows what is right for us because she is older and wiser than we are. I don't think she means to make trouble. She's a good mother and would never do anything like that. It looks to me like you're trying to create drama between us because you don't like my mother."

Nancy would get so angry, but she would try not to show it. If she did, Tom would get violent and attack her, as he had several times already. As a result of one such attack, she had suffered a concussion and a horrible headache. Talking about his mother was a NO-NO. Nancy knew that once the conversation was heading that way, she should stop talking. She complained to her mother, but there was little her mother was able to do. Nancy was prepared to endure all of it, because she was madly in love. Her mind was set on a better future and the idea that things would eventually change. She was hoping that Tom would one day wake up and realize how wrong he had been, especially once they had children. Nancy had no idea what a surprise life had in mind for her, one full of suffering and uncertainty.

II

It was a sunny spring day in May, and the flowers were blooming. Nancy gave a birth to beautiful baby girl. Jen was born a little bit underweight, but she was happy and healthy. Nancy had to spend two weeks at the hospital because Jen needed to gain the necessary weight before going home. Nancy had a long, painful labor. She had to endure pain for hours. The hospital had long corridors and high ceilings freshly painted walls in white. Nancy was using the corridors to walk back and forth because this was making the pain less. It was a nightmare because she had to tolerate the excruciating pain for so many hours. Her face was covered in tears, and she was feeling alone. There was no way for any relative to be present because the hospital rules did not allow it. That is why Tom was not allowed to be by Nancy's side. So, Tom did not have the opportunity to see their baby being born. He was out on a long drinking night with friends.

After the delivery, when the nurse called him at home, Tom was still recovering from the night before and it was hard for him to even talk. On the other side of the phone line, Nancy was recovering from the hard, painful night. She was given the phone to talk to Tom, and she told him, "Hi Tom, we have a healthy baby girl, and her name is Jen, just like your mother! Are you happy?"

Tom replied, "Of course I am. I wanted a girl in the first place. How are you doing?"

"I am fine, thank you," Nancy told him. "I had a hard time giving birth. I was in pain all night, and now I have no energy. The only thing I need now is a good sleep. How about you?"

"Oh, I had a wonderful night … a lot of food and drinks. I stayed up until two o'clock. Right now, I have a horrible headache, and I need a good sleep too!"

"I'm so happy for you," Nancy told him. "At least you did not have to see me suffer, and being outside with friends took your mind off me giving birth. Okay, I must go and rest! You do the same! Love you! Bye!"

"Love and kisses to both of you too!" Tom said, and they ended the call.

Nancy was taken to her room in a wheelchair, because she was not able to walk. She was allowed to rest as long as she wanted. The room where she was taken was big and sunny. She had to share it with several other mothers. The baby was taken to a special unit for underweight babies. The room was next to Nancy's, and she was able to see Jen through the window. The unit where Jen was taken was constantly monitored by the staff members. So she did not have to worry about anything. The babies were fed and taken care of. Jen was a lovely, tiny baby. Nancy was so thrilled with her, because she had wanted a girl so much.

Time passed by fast, because the baby was doing fine and gaining weight. Jen was given to her for breastfeeding every two hours. Soon, Nancy and Jen were ready to go home.

The whole family had been waiting for this moment, and they went to pick them up from the hospital. The hospital was surrounded by beautiful gardens full of flowers. It was a sunny and warm day. The birds were singing their happy songs. Everyone was smiling and so excited to meet the newborn.

It was a new thing at Tom's home. Jen changed the peace and quiet Tom's family had been accustomed to. In the beginning, Tom's mother helped out, but she slowly got tired of it. Nancy's mother was not the preferred person to be there and help out, because nobody there liked her. They tried to keep her as far away as possible, because she was a "bad influence" on Nancy. Everything that went wrong was Nancy's mother's fault. So, Nancy was left to cope alone with her new motherly duties. It was hard on her at the beginning, but she soon got used to it. When the weather allowed, Nancy would go and spend time with Jen in the nearby park. She would read a book until Jen had finished her nap.

That way she did not have to spend all of her time at home. She was able to meet other mothers there and make new friends as well. It was great opportunity for her to share her experiences with them and hear what they had to say.

It was a relief when her mother came to visit and help her. She would come during the day, when nobody but Nancy and Jen were home. Her mother would bring along her brother, John, who was a six-year-old at the time. Nancy was happy to have her family around. They made her feel comfortable in her skin. Her brother was a pleasant kid, and he would help by pushing Jen's stroller. He would ask Nancy, "Can I help with something? Please, please, I can do it."

Nancy would answer him, "Okay, John, but be careful. We don't want the baby to fall!"

John would say, "Oh, I will always be careful, and the baby will never fall." John was always careful and was a big boy with the attitude that he could do things. That is how the days passed for Nancy, and Jen was growing.

Nancy and Tom had a problem with Jen at bedtime. They would have to put Jen in her stroller and push her back and forth for hours before she would go to sleep. As young people, they needed to go out and to have friends over. Usually when they went out, they would take Jen to Nancy's house, because it was no problem to her mother to babysit Jen. She was so happy to have her at her home and take care of her and John. She loved being a mother and grandmother at the same time. The new man had no problem with having Jen around as well. They loved to stay home and have family time. This was a good thing for Tom and Nancy, because they knew they had someone they could count on every time they wanted to go out and have a good time with friends. Rose had a huge house with a garden. She would spend time with Nancy's brother and Jen in the yard, which was child proofed with high fences. Having a yard helped her because John was able to ride his bicycle until Jen went to sleep. Rose was having a great time being a mother and grandmother.

Tom's family was not anxious to babysit, because it interfered with their lifestyle. They wanted to be left alone most of the time, and only paid attention to the baby when they felt like it, and only for a short period of time. Even when Nancy and Tom had friends over for dinner, they had to feed Jen and put her to bed, because Tom's mother and father were too busy watching TV. Very often, Nancy was forced to stay with Jen for hours and only had time to say good-bye to her friends before they left. This was taking a toll on her emotionally, and it was creating tension in the family. She was not allowed to complain, because Tom always took his parents' side. It did not matter if they were right or wrong, because "wrong" was never a word that was allowed when it came to his parents. Nancy knew that if she complained, she could end up being slapped by Tom.

She had nobody to stand up for her. Her father had left her mother for another woman and was living far away. He would call from time to time, but Nancy and he never had the opportunity to go any deeper than a basic conversation. Usually, the whole family was listening in while she spoke to him. The reason for this was because the only phone they had was in the living room where Tom's family would spend the evenings watching the news. The person who would pick up the phone was Tom's mother. Nancy's father usually called in the evenings, so she had no privacy whatsoever. She had to act like everything is great. Nancy was sad, but her voice was never heard because nobody cared about how she felt. The only hope she had was that her father would help her get away by offering her a better place to live far away from Tom's parents. She had been thinking about it for a long time. It would be difficult for her to leave her mother and brother behind, but she had no choice. It seemed that every time there was a problem between Tom and Nancy, Tom's mother was to blame. Tom's mother made sure that Nancy paid for marrying her son against her will. Not listening to Jen was a crime, and everyone who dared do it paid dearly.

Tom's mother had no feelings whatsoever for little Jen. In her eyes, she was the granddaughter she never wanted from the woman she had never approved of. Jen hid this behind her constant smile, and the way she acted when everyone was around. She was pretty good at doing this. Compounded with Tom's drinking problem, the arguments between the young couple were becoming domestic violence disputes. Many times, Nancy had to leave the house bruised. Most times, when the arguments turned violent, Nancy's mother had to come and take Nancy and Jen to her home. Nancy did not want to be around Tom's family when she was upset about being attacked for no good reason. Tom's mother was constantly filling Tom with negative feelings. Jen was so manipulative, it was impossible for Nancy to compete with her. Jen had so much power over her son that Nancy's losing every battle against her was practically a sure thing. Nancy had learned that, but it was too late. She was young and inexperienced. Up until this time, she had never had to deal with people like her mother-in-law. She had been raised with a lot of love from her mother and grandmother. The fact that she had a baby was making everything so complicated, because she wanted Jen to have a father figure in her life. Divorce was unthinkable.

Nancy would tell her mother, "Mom, I know I should make changes in my life, because living like this is not right; but I don't want Jen to grow up and accuse me of not having allowed her to have a father. If I had my father here now, he would have the authority to talk to these people, and they would have never had the guts to treat me this way. They don't have any respect for you because you're a divorced woman, and they feel that you are less than they are. Besides, they're rich, and they think that what they're doing is right thing. They will never see us as being equal to them, and never give us any respect.

Nancy's mother would say, "I know it's hard not having your father around, but it's not right for you and the baby to live like this. It breaks my heart as a mother to watch you being verbally and physically attacked just because you have no way to stand up for yourself. We should try to find a solution. I don't want my daughter and granddaughter to be treated this way."

Nancy would respond, "Mother, please stay away from these people. They're good players and they always win, no matter what. They've never accepted you in their lives, because in their eyes, you're to blame as well for me marrying their son, because you didn't stop me from being with him. It's not like I was going to listen to you, but you're in the same boat as I am. I feel strongly that you should stay as far away from them as possible. Creating more tension won't help the situation. You'll end up being blamed."

"I guess you're right," Rose told Nancy one day. "I think the only choice we have is to try and talk to Tom. Maybe this would make things just a little bit better. What do you think?"

"I think that might be a good idea," Nancy said. "If we could convince him to stay with us for a little while at your house, this might bring him back to the person he used to be. A good influence always helps, but you never know."

The next day, Nancy asked Tom to go with her to visit her mother. It was a nice way for them to reconnect and have dinner like old times; but their visit was limited, unlike before. Tom's mother had been able to create a lot of tension and cut their connection down as short us she could, so nobody could interfere with her agenda. Rose was easy to talk to. As always, they had a lot of fun and talked about so many things. They were sitting in the kitchen having a delicious meal. The room was cozy and inviting. There was a small kitchen table with four chairs in the middle of the room. The windows had nice curtains with a design of red tulips. The smell of home cooking was contagious. Tom loved Rose's cooking. He liked her chicken soup a lot. She used special spices. He loved talking to her as well because she was fun to be around.

Rose said, "So, Tom, what do you think about staying here with us for a few days, so I can spend some time with you? I would be very happy to have you for a while, and I would love to spend some time around Jen."

Tom answered, "I think that's a good idea, and it would be a pleasure for us. I just have to talk to my mother. I don't feel that she would mind for us to be away for a while."

Nancy was relieved to learn the news, because she wanted to be as far away as possible from her mother-in-law for as long as she could. Tom had accepted the offer easily, but it was up to his mother to approve of it now. Nancy was hoping that she would not start attacking her mother and create a battlefield. Tom talked to his mother as soon as they got home. To Nancy's pleasant surprise, Jen was not in a mood to talk about Rose behind her back, and everything went the way Nancy and Tom had planned.

Tom and Nancy had a good time at Rose's house. Nancy and Rose would spend the day taking care of Jen and John. They were having a wonderful time together. There was no arguing between Nancy and Tom any longer, because the enabler was not around. It was nice, peaceful environment. Rose was preparing her authentic delicious meals every day. Tom was feeling happy. Everything went so well, but one week went by so fast and Nancy had to face her mother-in-law again. It was not too long before her life became the same nightmare again, full of drama and violence. One night she was forced to escape and go to a neighbor's house in the middle of the night. They were nice enough to open the door for her and let her use the phone. She called her father on the other side of the Atlantic and finally told him about the drama filled life she was living and the constant violence she was forced to endure. She poured her heart out to him.

"Dad, please help me. I am getting so tired of being slapped around and disrespected! Tom's mother hates me and treats me like garbage because she knows I don't have anyone around to defend me. If there is any way for you can make arrangements for us to come and live with you, I would appreciate it so much. Right now, it's the middle of the night and I'm calling you from my neighbor's house. They were nice enough to let me call you. I couldn't tell you until now what was happening here, because I always had witnesses around me. You have no idea how glad I am to be able to tell you everything about my life now. What do you think, Dad?"

"If that's the case, I am disappointed to hear it," Nancy's dad, Randy, said. "Tom never showed any sign that he would be the person you are telling me he is. This is a shock for me. And I always had the impression that Tom's parents were intelligent people. It never crossed my mind that you would be treated that way. I'll start working on it today and do everything possible to bring you and my granddaughter here. I'll talk to you tomorrow and tell you what steps to take. Good-bye, and don't worry!"

Nancy was relieved to hear that her father was willing to help. She had some doubt about it, because of his wife. Nancy had never liked her because she was the reason for her parents' divorce. In her eyes, she was no less an evil person than her mother-in-law, but she knew that this was the only way for her family to survive and have a happy life. Nancy was ashamed because she had been chased away in the wee hours from her home and had to leave eleven-month-old Jen behind because her drunk and out of control husband was slapping her around. His parents were there, but they never attempted to help her because they were enjoying every minute of it. To them, she was not worth even looking at, and she deserved the way their son was treating her, under their wise instructions. The neighbor man was nice enough to call Tom and tell him to come to their house for a little chat.

"So, Tom," the neighbor asked, "how do you feel about your wife running away from you in the middle in the night because you were beating her?"

Tom answered, "If she had not been being a bitch, she never would have put herself in this position. And nobody made her leave. She should have stayed home and taken what she deserved."

To this, the neighbor said, "I think that you are not capable of distinguishing right from wrong because of the alcohol you have in your blood, but I can tell you this: A real man would never lift a hand against his wife, because this makes him a half man. You should think about it tomorrow, and if you want to talk to me, I'll be here and happy to talk to you again. I think that you should calm down and go to bed. Your wife is scared to death. I'm sure your daughter is in the same condition as her mother, and you would see this if you woke her up. You should be ashamed of this evening's events. Good night, and talk to you tomorrow!"

Tom and Nancy went back home. They could not even look at each other. The whole situation had been so difficult and embarrassing. Tom held in his anger towards Nancy, because he knew that Nancy was prepared to go back to the neighbor's apartment.

The next day, things were quiet and calm. Everyone pretended that nothing had happened, including Nancy's mother-in-law, for whom this came naturally. She was smiling and not even asking any questions. She was proud of the way Tom was treating his wife and child. This charade was nothing new for Nancy, and she had no choice but go along with it. The only hope she had was that her father would help her out of this hell before something more serious happened.

Nancy called home. "Mother, Tom got drunk again and attacked me," she told Rose. "I had no choice but to run away and knock on the neighbor's door in the middle of the night. Nobody helped me when Tom was slapping me around. I couldn't even call you because he was holding me and throwing me around."

"I'm sorry, my dear daughter," Rose said. "This makes me so angry and sad, because I was not around to help you! Please tell me what I can do for you. Do you want me to come and get you?"

"No, Mom," Nancy said, "I'll come over as soon as I get Jen ready. I think we should spend the afternoon at home with you. Jen can take a nap there."

"See you soon, my dear!" Rose said.

Nancy was on her way to her mother's house with a broken heart and a sad face. She could not believe what was happening. She had never imagined that marrying the love of her life would cause such pain and sorrow. The domestic violence was even harder to endure. She had always thought she would never allow anybody to treat her that way. Tom was the last person she ever dreamed would be abusive towards her. Early in the relationship, she had told him stories about her father being abusive towards her mother. He would always assure her that he would never do such horrible things to any woman. Tom would tell Nancy, "I would never lift a hand against a woman. I feel that a real man should treat a lady with respect. There is nothing to worry about, Nancy; I love you so much that I would never hurt you." Nancy would feel very secure and desirable around Tom, and she never had a doubt about what he was telling her.

Nancy spent the afternoon at her mother's house and had a relaxing visit. Rose had set up a table and chairs outside her front door. The weather was warm. Nancy was feeling safe in the company of her mother. Nancy and Rose were sitting there, drinking coffee, and Nancy was telling her about the sadness she was forced to undergo. Her expression was full of sadness. Her heart was broken. The good thing was that she did not have to see her mother-in-law for a several hours. When she called Tom and told him where she was, he was not happy. He knew this would hurt his precious mother's feelings. Nancy felt as if she were in the army – she had rules to follow. When it started to get dark outside, she had to pack her bags and head back to "jail." Everyone would be coming home from work.

Nancy was unpacking her bags when Tom came to the door. He was in the worst possible mood and ready to argue. His mother was in the same mood. She knew Nancy had visited her mother and had told her about the previous night. Nancy knew what was going to happen after Tom's routine night of drinking.

After dinner, Tom started in on Nancy. "So, did you tell your mother about what you did last night? Did you tell her how embarrassing it was for all of us – you knocking on the neighbor's doors in the middle of the night?" His voice became louder. "She took your side, of course, because she's your mother! That's why I don't want you to go there and tell her what's going on here. Maybe you should start to do what my mother and I tell you. Did you hear what I said, Nancy?"

Nancy defended herself, saying, "I feel that you don't even hear what is coming from your mouth. Visiting my mother should not be an issue for you or anybody else."

Tom became angrier. "Talking back to me instead of listening is not going to improve the situation. You should listen and agree with me. When I say you are wrong, it means you are wrong! And I would never agree with you when it comes to your mother. End of this discussion. Tomorrow, you will stay here. You will not leave the house! I'll be calling you and checking on you." Tom did not want to show any guilt about his actions. It was difficult for Nancy to accept that he was so unwilling to be civilized and take responsibility for his behavior. Nancy had no choice. She did not want to be attacked again. The best thing to do was to go to bed and forget about everything. Even so, she felt angry because she knew she had not done anything wrong.

The next day, Nancy's father called and told her the good news. He had been able to arrange for them to live with him until they could get a place on their own. This was the best news for her, but at the same time, the saddest. Her mother and brother meant so much to her, but this was the only solution. She had to break away from the slavery she was in. For the first time in a long time, Nancy was experiencing the feeling of being happy.

She called her mother right away and told her the good news. "Mother, Mother, guess what? My dad called today and told me that he has made arrangements for us to go and live with him. Oh, Mom, I have the best feeling that things will turn for the better once we leave my mother-in-law's. She'll be far away, and we'll finally be able to have our own place. Are you happy for me, Mom? I'll miss you and John so much, but you can come and visit. What do you think?"

"I am happy for you and sad at the same time," Rose said, "because I don't want you to be so far away from me. The only thing that makes me feel better is the fact that you are happy and this will stop the never ending drama in your life and mine – because I suffer as much as you do. I don't want to see my daughter beaten every day and living the life I had to live when your father and I had problems. If this will improve your situation, I want you to go!"

"Thank you, Mother," Nancy said. "Your support and kind words mean a lot to me."

Nancy could not wait for Tom to come back from work to tell him the news. He was happy about it. But when his mother got back from work and learned the news, she was not. This was not unexpected, and it did not surprise anyone. Being in control of her son's family and torturing Nancy were the greatest pleasures for her, and she was losing these. It was not easy in the beginning, because Jen kept trying to find reasons to keep her son hanging on her skirt. Tom attacked Nancy several times before their departure, but Nancy stayed strong. The thought that their situation was going to improve soon was reason enough for her to keep her head up.

III

The big day slowly approached, and Nancy, Tom, and Jen left the country and the troubled home. It was a long and overwhelming trip. Everybody was happy because this was a new beginning for the whole family. Nancy's father was waiting, along with his second wife, at the airport. Nancy was happy to see him. She had not seen him for a long time. He took them to his house, and they had a great time catching up. He had prepared a welcome dinner. The food was wonderful and everyone was very friendly. They were living in a two-bedroom apartment. One of the bedrooms was prepared for Tom, Nancy and Jen. Everything inside the house looked brand new. The bed was covered with white sheets and a blanket. Next to the bed, there was a baby crib for Jen. There were new baby clothes on the top of the crib. They had to live with Nancy's father's family for a short time, until Tom could find a job and they could move into an apartment.

Nancy was very grateful to her father, and everything was going so great ... but not for long. Once in his own home, Tom started gradually going back to his old ways of drinking and being abusive towards Nancy. Jen again had to witness scenes of her father drunk and attacking her mother. Tom had no mercy towards Nancy even in Jen's presence. One night at 3:00 am, Nancy had to call her dad to ask him for help. She cried, "Please, Dad, come and help me! Tom is so drunk, and I have no control over him. I want you to come and talk to him. I can't talk to him. He won't listen to me, and he's hitting me. He's threatening to take Jen with him and I'll never get to see him or her again."

Nancy's father said, "I'm coming, and I'll do whatever I can to help. Don't talk to him anymore until I get there. Try to calm the situation down and stay away from him."

Nancy said, "Thank you, Dad. I'm so sorry for waking you up. I'll be waiting for you!"

Randy arrived at their apartment cross. He had never expected Tom to have the guts to lift his hand to his daughter while they lived close to him. Tom had already left. He was afraid to face him. Nancy's was badly bruised, and she was crying hysterically. Jen was by her side shaking and scared to death. Randy decided that the best thing to do was to call the police and report what had happened. The whole house was a huge mess. There were pieces of glass scattered all over the floor. Everything was out of place. There were obvious signs that someone out of control had created the scene. It was extremely disturbing and, at the same time, sad for Nancy's father to witness this. He loved his daughter and granddaughter, and this was the last thing he wanted them to have to go through. Nancy's face was badly bruised, and her arm was covered with scratches. Good thing was that she was not hurt more seriously. She and Jen were sobbing. Nancy's father was angry and did not know how to make things better for her and Jen.

The police came to Nancy's apartment and saw the bruises on Nancy's face and hands. They took pictures of the bruises and scratches she had all over her arms and hands. The scratches were a result of her trying to defend herself. Nancy told the police the whole story of how Tom had got drunk and had started yelling and screaming for no reason. He had a habit of starting an argument whenever he decided to. It was not hard for him to find a way to start a fight.

Nancy told the police the story of what had happened that night: "Tom came home from work. Before dinner, he had several drinks. After dinner, he had a few more drinks. Then suddenly, he jumped up and decided to start an argument about something. I told him to stop, and he decided to leave the house and drive somewhere. So I tried to stop him, and he started to push me and then he hit me because he wanted me to let go of him. Finally, I couldn't hold on to him any longer, and he broke free and ran out the door.

"Jen followed him, and I ran after them. He picked up Jen and ran out into the parking lot with her and got into the car. I tried to open the door, but it was locked. He was threatening to run away with her and never come back. So, I started to beg him to let her go, and she jumped out of the car. Then we went back to the apartment and I called my dad."

One of the police officers asked, "Do you have any idea where he might be?"

Nancy answered, "No, I do not know."

Then the officer asked her, "Can you tell us what he looks like and what kind of a car he's driving?"

Nancy answered, "He drives a black Honda, and he's five, seven and has dark brown hair."

The officer said, "Thank you. If he shows up, call us right away. He has no business here until the judge decides what's going to happen with him."

Nancy, Jen, and Randy were all speechless. They could not believe what had just happened. This was a wake-up call for Nancy's dad about what Nancy had to bear when she was living in Europe, far away from him. They talked for a little while, and then they got a call from the police informing them that they had found Tom sleeping in his car. They were taking him to jail, and the police gave them the option of picking up the car, so they would not have to pay for towing.

Tom spent the night in jail, and the judge ordered him to stay away from Nancy for a period of two weeks. During this time, he was secretly calling and apologizing. Nancy was busy running the business, spending time with Jen, and housework. She was disappointed and hurt because there was not much of a difference in Tom's behavior. This realization was eating at her soul and making her feel hopeless and helpless. Tom did not show much affection for her or Jen. He had not changed. The only difference was that they had the means to take vacations and buy a nice car. Tom was a good businessman, and they had been able to get into a good business. It was not easy for them in the beginning, but they both worked hard for a long time. They were able to buy the dream house they had always wanted, but their relationship was like a rollercoaster. When the great recession hit the country, things got even worse.

IV

Nancy was extremely devoted to her family, and she never gave up on Tom. Although she knew that everything that Tom did impacted Jen as well, she was still hoping that things would change. Things did change for the better after her mother-in-law's death. But Tom was already so filled with his mother's negative feelings towards her that it was impossible to change him. She was so used to suffering because of Tom's mother's influence on her family, and she felt her presence at all times.

As time passed, Tom started turning into his parents, and his and Nancy's relationship took another downward turn. He did not feel the urge to help improve their financial situation; just the opposite. His father was getting older and wanted Tom to come and stay with him. Nancy did not know how to react to that idea. She wanted to go somewhere and clear her head. On the one hand were her mother and her mother's boyfriend; and on the other, her husband and his father. The bills were piling up like a mountain, but she was determined to save money for her and Tom to go on a much needed vacation.

Nancy had managed to save $1,300, and she told Tom about her intentions to take time off and the money she had saved. Tom was not happy to learn about her plans, because he wanted to go and visit his dad, and he even demanded the money be given to him for that purpose. Nancy was devastated to hear this because she had been hoping he would have a different reaction. The money she had was enough to pay for a vacation to Hawaii and still have some spending money for the trip. The idea was to take a vacation so they could recharge and see what they could do to save the dream house they had waited for so long for and somehow improve their marriage, but Tom wanted Nancy to cancel the vacation. Tom's priority was his "needy" father.

"I have to go and see my father now," Tom insisted. "If I don't, I don't know if I will have another chance to see him!"

Nancy reminded him, "I gave you the choice, either come with me on vacation or go to see your dad, and you chose to come with me. What do you want me to do now, give up my vacation and the money I put aside for it?"

Nancy knew that Tom only cared about the money she had saved. She was irritated and heartbroken about that. There was little she could do about it. She just had to endure the harsh reality of her life. She had to pretend that everything was fine and that nothing had happened. It was just Tom's insensitive way of ignoring Nancy's attempts to bring them closer together.

Jen was old enough to see the pain in Nancy's eyes. She was also impacted by her father's drinking and abuse. After hearing the two of them arguing, Jen told Nancy, "Mom, don't you get tired of these arguments? Why don't you just try to ignore him? You can't change him. He'll be doing this for the rest of his life. This is the way he is."

Nancy agreed with Jen, saying, "I know. You're right, but it's not easy to bow your head when you feel that you need to say something."

"Mom," Jen said, "listen. Please stop paying attention to him – for my sake. I'm sick of the fighting … and how am I supposed to have a normal life when I have to see you two fighting all the time?"

That moved Nancy. "Yes," she agreed, "I know you're right. Things need to change around here, and I promise you I'll do my best to stop fighting with him. One thing that could help your father and I get along better would be for us to go on this vacation alone together. I would like it if you would help me make it possible by watching things here while we're gone."

"Mom," Jen said, "you know I'll take care of everything while you two are gone. I promise, no parties – and I'll run the business. You won't have any worries."

It was going to be hard for Nancy to leave Jen behind to go on vacation – and also her precious dog that she loved so much. Nancy felt frustrated by Tom's manipulations. But she knew it was not good to torture Jen with the constant arguing. So, she decided to ignore Tom's craziness and his efforts to start arguments. The business was in big trouble, and things were not improving. Nancy did not pressure herself to try to do the impossible. She just did what she could and hoped that things would somehow turn out all right.

Tom, for his part, was secretly hoping to get his way and make Nancy give him the money she had. But he made it a point to not show any signs of worry about getting his way. Hiding what he was thinking was now a habit with him. He had been building his life behind Nancy's and Jen's backs by secretly sending money all the extra money the business had brought in to his parents. His mother had masterminded of all this while she was alive. This was her way of destroying their lives, no matter how far away they were from her. She never allowed them a minute of peace. Everything was under her constant guidance, and Tom followed all of her orders.

She had used Nancy and Jen for an excuse to prove her point about having Tom send them the money. "Son," she would say, "I am worried that these two are spending your money on clothes and unnecessary things. I believe it would be better for you to send it to us, so I can save it for you. This way, you do not have to give money to them, and you do not have to think about your future being destroyed. I am really disappointed about their spending. Please, Son, listen to your mother." This was a great way for Tom's mother to plant more negative feelings towards his wife and daughter and make his home a toxic environment, full of drama.

Shortly after her death, Tom's dad started calling him at one o'clock in the morning complaining about not being able to pick up his prescription and wanting Tom to go back to Europe and take care of him. This took a huge toll on Nancy and Jen, because it made Tom feel extremely pressured. He was constantly preoccupied with his father's situation, and everything he did suffered as a result. The business was going downhill, the family relations were poor, and they were buried in debt. Tom's dad was an alcoholic and he had become obsessed with women. The only thing he did all day was drink. He would spend money like crazy. All of his money was going to alcohol and cigarettes. His house was looking like a tavern. Everywhere there was the smell of smoke and alcohol, but there was no way to talk him out of his bad habit. He was stubborn to the bone and would not listen to anyone, but himself.

V

The day of their departure for Hawaii came, and Tom and Nancy packed their bags. Tom complained the whole way to the airport and continued complaining at the airport. There were a lot of people in the airport waiting to board the plane. Everyone there was blissful and smiling. The atmosphere was amazing and was starting to make Nancy feel much better because of the positive vibe around her. The only person who seemed to have a problem was Tom. He was complaining to Nancy. "Where are we going now? Everything is a huge mess around us. I do not know how you could have the nerve to spend money and feel good about going away. I am just speechless."

Nancy tried to ignore him as much as possible. She called Jen. Jen was on her first day at her new job at the family business. Since she was working alone there, Nancy was able to call her several times. Nancy was trying to ignore her grumpy husband's constant nagging. She was already imagining the beauty of the sea and the peace and quiet that she had been looking forward to for months. She told Tom, "Try to relax and pretend that you deserve this vacation! I know things are bad, but you need a vacation. You can't go on like this. Maybe things will take a turn for the better while we are gone. In any case, you'll clear your head and think of some ways to cope with the situation. I know it's hard, but believe me, this is a good move. And don't worry, Jen and Jason will take care of everything while we're gone."

They had just hired Jason, and he was a good employee. He was very helpful. Tom and Jason had a good relationship based on trust. Tom needed someone like Jason around to help him with the business. Tom was feeling more secure and confident. Whenever Tom needed to leave the business, Jason was there. He knew Jason loved the idea of being a boss when he was not around.

As soon as Tom and Nancy arrived at the airport in Hawaii, everything seemed fine. Tom was starting to loosen up a bit. The music in the plane changed to a wonderful island rhythm. All of the passengers were in a vacation mood. When they stepped out of the plane, the fresh, warm island breeze and the smell of flowers was incredible. It was hard even for the most stubborn person not to forget about his bad temper. The warm breeze made Tom feel more relaxed. He even took the initiative to rent a car. It was a huge surprise for Nancy, but she was taking it one day at the time. Seeing Tom get excited about the trip was not something she wanted to take for granted. She was trying to put their depressing reality behind them and enjoy the beautiful surroundings of Hawaii. Tom and Nancy drove along the road by the ocean. The view was spectacular and the warm wind was blowing through the car windows. They were talking to each other like they had never had a problem.

Nancy asked, "So, Tom, what do you think about my choice? Do you still stand by your position about me being irresponsible and not considering the financial situation we are in? I would love to know your opinion about it."

Tom replied, "I feel great, but I'm still not ready to say how I feel about all this. I want to admit that this is the most beautiful, peaceful place I have ever seen. Coming here was not the worst thing, after all."

Soon they arrived at the resort where they had reservations. The place was right by the ocean. It looked like an oasis. There were tropical flowers and trees everywhere. The scent in the air was indescribable. Nancy and Tom were greeted by a welcoming gatekeeper. He smiled and gave them directions to the hotel where they had reservations. They drove to the reception desk at the newly build hotel by the ocean. The receptionist was friendly and very talkative.

As soon as they got their key for their room, they were taken to a nearby building by a porter. Their room was located in an old building that smelled like mold. Nancy got nervous because she did not want Tom to be disappointed. The last thing she needed was another argument. They walked down the hallway carrying their luggage, anxious to see the room. It turned to be a disappointment. The smell of mold in the room was even stronger than in the hallway. Nancy could not hold in her anger.

"Tom," she said, "I can't sleep in this room. There is no way I am staying here."

Tom replied, "Don't worry, we can open the balcony door and the smell will go away."

"No, no, no," Nancy insisted. "We are going back to the reception desk and demanding a new room – a clean one worth the money we paid. I'm not going to tolerate this room. It will only make me sick and destroy any chance of enjoying our trip. We are here on vacation, and I feel this is the right thing to do."

Soon Nancy and Tom were carrying their luggage back to the lobby. Nancy went to talk to the friendly receptionist who had given them the key to the moldy room. "Excuse me, Miss. There is no way that we can stay in that room. I got sick from the smell of mold. You should not allow anybody to stay there. I even started coughing from it. We would appreciate it if you gave us another room."

The Receptionist answered, "Okay, Miss, I'll let the manager know. He'll be with you shortly. Please take a seat in the lobby."

The manager quickly appeared and offered them a villa. He told them, "I won't charge you any extra for the villa, even though they're a bit more expensive."

Tom told him that they wanted to have a room in the new hotel. The manager said, "I won't be able to accommodate you in this building without your paying extra for it."

"No," Tom said, "I'm not paying a penny extra. It's not my fault that the room we paid for was not what we expected."

The manager insisted, saying, "I am sorry, sir, but I'm giving you the option of a villa without any additional fee."

Tom thought about it and said, "We'd like to see the villa before we give our final decision. Is this okay with you?"

"Yes, I'll be here waiting," the manager answered.

Nancy and Tom were seated on a small shuttle with their luggage and taken by a staff member to the area where the villas were located. It was a nice area with gardens and small bungalows attached to one another. Each of the bungalows had a private patio with a table and chairs. The smell of flowers was amazing and the view of the ocean was indescribable. The villas were not new, but they had been recently remodeled. They needed a bit of housekeeping, but Tom liked the privacy. They were surrounded by a beautiful garden covered with tropical flowers and Hawaiian trees. Nancy was not thrilled with the hygiene of the villa, but Tom was the one she wanted to be pleased with the accommodations. So, she settled for the villa. As soon as they were left alone in the room, they started to unpack their swimsuits, and soon headed to the ocean. It was almost five in the afternoon, but the sun was shining high in the sky and the birds were singing.

Tom told Nancy, "Oh, I can't believe it; it's five a clock and the sun is still so strong."

Nancy said, "Don't forget, we're in the tropics. Things are different here."

They walked along the small path that led to the beach. The beach was only two minutes from their room. They were awed to see that the beach was as beautiful as in a storybook. It was lined with palm trees with strange fruit hanging from the branches. Nancy and Tom saw a young couple heading into the water, and Nancy decided to follow them. As soon as she got into the water, she asked the young woman, "Where are you from?"

She answered, "I am from Germany."

Nancy asked, "What brings you all the way here?"

The woman answered, "My husband and I just got married, and we decided to spend our honeymoon here."

Nancy asked, "Did you go somewhere else before here? Did you visit any other places?"

The German woman answered, "Yes, we went to Las Vegas, San Francisco, and L.A."

Nancy continued with her questions: "Did you like those places?"

The woman answered, "Yes, a lot. It was so much fun for us."

They continued talking for a while, then Nancy got out of the water and Tom decided to go for a swim. Nancy was feeling on the top of the world. She had been dreaming about this vacation for so long. She was surprised by the beauty of this island. This was everything she had wanted for Tom and her.

Tom and Nancy stayed at the beach to watch the sunset. It was so beautiful and peaceful, and the only noise was from a bird singing in a nearby palm tree.

Nancy asked Tom, "Did you ever imagine that I was going to take you to see such a peaceful place?"

Tom replied, "No, I have never imagined in my wildest dreams that there was place like this. This is everything I could ask for."

"I am very proud of myself," Nancy said, "because I made you happy. This is the kind of place I knew you would love to visit to take a break and forget about all our troubles."

Tom said, "I wish I could say the same, but it isn't going to be easy. There are so many things that are hard not to think about."

"I know," Nancy said, "we are in so much debt. But let's try to enjoy the short time we have here. Maybe something good will come of it."

Nancy and Tom were in so much pain. It was hard to cope with everything. This vacation was kind of like a pill. In a place like this, the days went by fast. Tom and Nancy spent most of the time at the beach. The evenings were a time to sit on the porch and have something to drink and watch the stars in the sky. They enjoyed the warm breeze coming from the ocean and the beautiful surroundings.

VI

Their vacation was almost over, and they had to go back home and face reality. It was hard for them to leave such a beautiful and peaceful place. It was a place that had given them the opportunity to rejuvenate and unload their pail of troubles for a short period of time. The last day of their vacation was filled with mixed feelings. They wanted to enjoy the few hours left in paradise. Things were not so good back home. Nancy and Tom returned the rental car at the airport and unloaded their luggage. They had enough time to have lunch at a restaurant before boarding the airplane and heading back home.

Nancy was trying to forget about what awaited them back home by asking random questions. "Do you think that we should come here for another vacation next year?"

Tom replied, "Oh that would be the best thing ever."

Nancy asked, "Let's see how things work out, and let's definitely think about coming back next year."

Tom was deeply depressed, and now he didn't even hear what Nancy was saying. The whole world was falling apart around him, and it was hard for him to even imagine that something good might happen. He told Nancy, "It's going to take a miracle for things to get better. I'm so worried about everything, and right now, I don't want to think about it. Let's enjoy the last few hours we have left before we land home in Denver."

Nancy replied with a smile on her face, "You are right. Let's enjoy it and remember these good times when we get home. We're going to have plenty of time to work on everything. "

As Tom finished his lunch, he tried to pretend that he wasn't worried about the troubles back home. It was almost time to find their terminal and prepare to leave the most wonderful place in the world.

Their flight landed in Denver on time, but there was a problem with the luggage compartment on the plane. Tom and Nancy had to sit and wait at the airport along with all the other passengers. Jen was waiting for them in her car at the call zone. It was not a pleasant experience for anyone. All of the passengers were complaining because they wanted to get home and rest.

Finally, one of the employees announced, "It is going to take at least two hours to get the cargo door open. If you want, you can go home and your luggage can be delivered. If you would like your luggage to be delivered, please go to the desk and fill out the form."

Then suddenly, there was announcement that the cargo door had been opened and that everyone would be able to pick up their luggage shortly. Everyone was relieved to get the news. Nancy called Jen, who was tired from the long wait in the car. "Jen," Nancy said, "they just told us that our luggage is on its way, and we can go home pretty soon. Your dad and I are going to call you when you can meet us at the exit."

Soon after the announcement, the belt started to run and people started to disappear through the door. Nancy and Tom got their luggage and finally left to meet their daughter. Their beloved dog, Pete, was in the car. Pete was wagging his tail unstoppably and licking their hands. It was a nice September night. It was not cold yet, and they were happy to be on their way home. It was already dark outside. There weren't any cars on the road, because everyone was already at home. The windows of the car were open and fresh air was coming inside.

The house had been kept nice and clean, and Nancy was impressed by the neatness. She did not expect this, so it was a very pleasant surprise for her. It was a sign that her daughter was already mature and that her party days were over.

"Oh, Jen," she said, "I'm so happy to see our home in this condition. And you didn't have any parties while we were gone?"

"Mom, I only have a few close friends – not the whole world like the last time. I'm already over that phase when kids used to come over uninvited!"

"Okay, I guess I can have more getaways with your father, then. Finally, we can relax and not worry about our home being trashed."

Everyone was already tired from the long wait at the airport and ready for bed. Jen was happy because she was no longer responsible for the dog and all of the house chores. Nancy was doing a little unpacking because she needed some of her things. She surprised Jen with a little present.

VII

The good times were already behind them, and Tom was ready to face reality again. He was preparing to go and see how things were going with the business. Nothing had changed during his absence. Business was bad, but he was willing to work on it. The recession was not coming to the end – it was doing the opposite. Tom had other problems besides the house and the business. His father wanted him to bring the whole family back to Europe, because he was feeling alone and needed them to take care of everything for him. The pressure on Tom was making it impossible for him to dedicate all of his attention to the critical situation he faced.

It was too much for him to handle all of the problems and make the right decisions to improve the situation. He had the bank to deal with. He needed to work with them to make his payments more affordable, so the whole family could keep a roof over their heads. Then there was the problem of business being slow, and their income not being adequate to meet their expenses. Nancy was doing everything she could to help. She was dealing with the banks and, at the same time, working on the rest of the problems.

Nancy suggested, "We should open another business, so we can have more options!"

Tom agreed, "I think that's a very good idea!"

Nancy and Tom started to see the bad situation from a more favorable perspective, which gave them hope for the future. They needed some positive vibrations around them. The idea of starting a new business was like a new beginning. Nancy got busy planning and preparing everything for the new business and the house. It was overwhelming at times, and she was often tired and frustrated. It seemed impossible to prioritize which obstacles to tackle first.

Tom was so absorbed in his father's situation that he could not think straight. His father kept calling him and asking him to come back and live with him. He was not the slightest bit concerned about Tom's immediate problems or whether his family had any objections. It was impossible for Tom to explain to him that he had a family, and a business and a house that were in trouble. The only thing important to Tom's father was his problem of not having any company and feeling alone. He was an old stubborn coward, and his name was Larry. He was very spoiled and used to having someone to take care of him. He could not even make himself a salad. Most widows his age were doing fine on their own, but he was not. His health was bad because of his continual drinking and smoking. All of these bad habits were impacting his ability to cope with the outside world.

He was having a hard time finding his way home after going to the store or taking a short walks. At the same time, he was pressuring Tom to send him money without even considering Tom and Nancy's situation. Tom had to send him money because he was so pushy, and the only way to get him to stop calling was to send him money that he did not need. He would tell Tom, "I want to spend the rest of what is left of my life being able to do what I want. I don't need anyone telling me what I should do. If I am going to die tomorrow, I want to die with money in my pocket. So, please Son, make sure that my last wish is fulfilled."

Tom would reply: "Don't worry, Dad, I'll make sure that your last wish is taken care of. That is why I am your son, to make sure you die happy. But there is one thing I will not be able to do for you, and that is come back and stay with you. I cannot leave my family right now." After a conversation like this, Tom would feel emotionally drained. His face showed that he was in a lot of pain. It was additional luggage for the family, having an inconsiderate relative to whom it was impossible to explain that there were problems that were more pressing than his own.

Tom was not able to do what his father was asking, because he had so many other things to take care of. His father had his daughter from his first marriage there, and she was the one who would make his call for help for him. In addition, he had the maid who had been taking care of the cleaning and laundry for several years. His situation was not that bad, but Tom's parents had held power over him all his life. They were the ones who had been laying down the rules in his house, and he had always listened to them without objection. It was torture for everybody, but his parents always took first position no matter what.

Several months passed and Christmas came. Tom and Nancy were still struggling with their financial problems. The bank was uncooperative, and it was getting extremely hard to keep up with all of their bills. Jen was working, but she was only making enough to cover her own expenses. A lot of people were losing their homes, and it was sad and scary. There was not any improvement anywhere. It was a big struggle to find a job. Millions of people were unemployed, and the demand for jobs was huge. So many companies had to let their employees go because they could not afford to keep them any longer.

It was a sad Christmas for many people. Even at Christmastime, people were spending significantly less than usual because uncertainty was a scary thing for everyone. Tom was trying to make things even more complicated because presents were never something he thought were necessary. For Nancy, Christmas was a very important holiday and presents were something they absolutely had to have under the tree. The good thing was that so many things were on sale because of the bad economy. So, she was somehow able to buy a present for everyone.

Nancy was the decorator at the house. It was a great pleasure for Nancy to make the whole house look like a little Christmas village. She had everything from the shiny, sparkly, artificial flowers for the vases to little Christmas figures. The Christmas tree was tastefully decorated as well. Nancy liked the color silver, so all of the decorations were of this color. Around the Christmas tree, there was a small train that went around in circles. Nancy loved her home so much, and she wanted it to look perfect. Perfection was her thing, and she did everything she could to show it and make all of her loved ones happy. Jen loved to watch and help her. Tom was responsible for the yard decorations. He put up the lights on the doors and bushes. He enjoyed doing his part as well.

Christmas day was almost here, and everybody was nervous. Tom told Nancy, "I don't know how we are going to be able to pay for everything next year if we don't have a second income. Probably, I'll be in a hospital because of the unbearable pressure we had to go through this year."

Nancy was trying to be more optimistic, as always. She told Tom, "Don't worry about next year, Tom. Let's be grateful for what we were able to keep this year and hope for the best."

Tom replied, "I guess. As always, you are right. We should be more optimistic about the future. We should make a Christmas wish."

It was early in the morning, and the whole family was opening their presents, including the dog and the cat. Everybody was happy and full of joy. Like every Christmas, Tom was the one who prepared the dinner. The menu was the same every year: turkey and sauerkraut. It was a special dish they had been having since they were kids back in Poland. The whole house was full of the delicious smell of home cooking. It was nice and warm. The fireplace was making crackling noises. Nancy was making her homemade bread. She put up the decorations and made sure there was a CD of Christmas songs in the CD player. Jen, as always, was busy enjoying her new additions to her closet. She was the one who got the most presents.

And, as usual, she was the one asking, "Mom, when is the dinner going to be ready? I'm getting really hungry!"

"Soon, my dear," Nancy answered, "but you'll have to eat something before then. It's too early for dinner, and you should have lunch."

"But, Mom, I want to have some of what's baking right now. It smells so good!"

"No, Jen," Nancy told her, "you should wait for the dinner to be ready, and we should all sit down and have Christmas dinner together."

"Okay, then," Jen said, "I can have something small for lunch and wait."

"Thank you, Jen. I know you can do it."

When the dinner was ready, everyone was helping to set the table. As always, the turkey and sauerkraut were fabulous. Tom had even made homemade sauerkraut. Store-bought sauerkraut was extremely sour, and it was not as tasty as the Tom's homemade sauerkraut. Everyone was at the table having Christmas dinner and trying to forget the troubles surrounding them. It was time for everyone to forget and put the past behind them as much as they could.

VIII

The holidays over, it was time to start the New Year with the hope that a solution to their financial problems could be found. Neither of the banks was open to negotiation, and everyone in the family was getting nervous. Business was the same, and they had to find a way to cope with the harsh reality as soon as possible. At the same time, Tom's dad, Larry, was complaining that he felt extremely alone and needed Tom to come and keep him company. Tom's sister, Sue, wrote him a letter telling him that his dad needed a companion.

One night she called. "Hi, Tom. I want to tell you that I feel strongly that it is time for you to come and take care for Dad. I can't handle this responsibility any longer. He is too much work, and I can't do it by myself. Let's not forget that he is your father as well. I have my family responsibilities also, but I always find time for him."

It was not easy for Tom to be put in a position like this, so he had to make a decision right away. Things were really serious. Larry was losing his mind at times. It looked like his bad habit was destroying important functions in his brain, and as a result, he was getting in trouble. He was not thinking rationally anymore and could not distinguish right from wrong.

Sue told Tom that when he went out, he did not remember his way back and very often got lost. She also told him that around Christmastime, he invited some people to his house for a drink and they robbed him. Tom's father did not remember what had happened because he lost consciousness for a little while. When he woke up, the guests were already gone. He also did not even remember who the people were who had been at the house. The only thing he remembered was that when he woke up, he looked around the apartment and noticed that everything was out of order and a lot of things were missing. Consequently, he decided to alert the neighbors about it. So he went out into the hallway and started screaming, "I've been robbed! Please, somebody, help me!"

He screamed until some of his neighbors showed up and went into his apartment to see what had happened. They asked him if he wanted to let the police know about it, but he refused. But, he did tell them that some important documents were missing, along with $4,000. The whole story sounded unbelievable. Tom had his suspicions about his sister, Sue, who was quite interested in the apartment and the piece of land that had been given to Tom. There was no doubt that this time Tom had to go and find out what had happened. He could not take any chances with the situation.

Tom's trip made their budget even tighter, but Tom could not do anything about it. He felt so pressured, because he had to spend money he did not have and could not afford. The night before his flight, Nancy and Tom got into a fight because Tom got drunk and started causing problems. He took all of his anger out on Nancy. He started screaming at Nancy, "You are the one who makes me drink, and everything is your fault. If it you were not for you, we wouldn't be in this situation. Calling your mother every day is one of the problems. You shouldn't talk to her every day."

Nancy was fed up with all of his accusations that she has been listening to for twenty years. She was in agony. She told him, "You are leaving tomorrow, and you should be ashamed of yourself. How could you be so insensitive and obnoxious at a time like this? I don't know what your reaction will be in the morning when you wake up and realize what a jerk you were!"

The person who suffered the most from all this arguing was Jen. She had never had the parents she wanted and had been entitled to her whole life. The reason was their constant disagreements about Tom's parents and their needs, and what could be done to improve their situation. Everything was about them, and nothing else mattered. Jen needed her parents to find time for her and to pay attention to her for once. Instead, her life was consumed by her being an adult and being a referee in their never ending arguments. So she started to pull away from them by spending more time at her friends' houses. It was a good thing. She had the chance to see how other people interacted, and how other people who had elderly parents did not constantly argue about them. She shared her observations with Tom and Nancy, and told them that spending so much time worrying about their parents' problems was stupid and that she could not believe they could not realize that.

"You argue so much about your parents that you don't have the chance to live your own lives," Jen told them. "When are you two going to live for yourselves for once? Can't you understand that you are missing out on all the wonderful things life has to offer? Look at yourselves! Half of your lives are gone, and you still continue to care more about other people than you do about yourselves. Do you think your parents care about you? I don't think so. And when exactly are you going to have time for me? You've never asked me what I want to do or who I want to be. When are you going to be the parents, and let me be the child? Can you answer this question?"

Nancy and Tom sat quietly and listened. They knew she was right, but it was impossible to make so many changes at once. But at least she gave them something to think about.

Nancy said, "I know we are lousy parents, and we've never paid enough attention to you. But the problem we have is so deeply rooted that I think it's impossible to get rid of overnight. You have every right to be angry with us. At this time, I would be willing to help you with your career choice and listen to what you have to say. I love you with all of my heart, and I can promise you that I'll do whatever it takes to help you get to where you want to be. The only thing I can't promise you is that our arguments will stop."

The next morning, they had to wake up at 5:00 AM. Tom's flight was at 8:00 AM. Nancy was still upset, and she was not open to any conversation. Tom was acting like a small child who had made a booboo in his diaper. It took forty-five minutes to get to the airport from their home. During the whole trip, there was silence in the car. They arrived on time at the drop-off area and did not even kiss each other good-bye, even though they were not going to see each other for twenty days. The only thing Nancy was able to say after the night before was, "Have a nice trip."

Nancy was so angry about the way Tom had behaved the night before that she did not even realize it when he left to enter the airport. She just wanted to go home and forget about him. Tom's drinking was still creating a lot of problems and tension around the house and in every aspect of their lives. His disrespect towards Nancy and Jen was out of control. Tom's parents had been using Tom to their advantage and manipulating and milking him for money for years.

Nancy had her suspicions about his stealing money and sending it to his parents. When she was able to start to manage the money for the business, she was convinced of it. It was obvious to her that all these years she had been badly betrayed. Her money had been used to pay to support the people who hated her and had talked about her behind her back since she and Tom had met. The sad part was that Tom was so foolish that he had fallen for it. Nancy had been naïve and had not been willing to believe that the only man she had ever known and loved – the man she had been willing to put up with for so many years with his drinking problem, violent behavior, and total disrespect – had been robbing her. It was a shocking and painful situation. She had endured everything for the sake of her family.

The other, more pressing problem for her at that moment was that she had no money or career to enable her to leave Tom and start a new life. Everything she had worked for had been taken from her, and she had no choice but to work on their financial and business problems. Otherwise, they would end up on the street. She could not go back and live with her mother, because her mother was living with another crazy person who had been torturing her and Nancy's brother because he wanted her to leave her house to him. On the other hand, Tom would be quite happy to live with his dad, because he did not have to work at all. The money he had stolen and the rent from the land he owned would be enough to cover his expenses.

Tom's dad was ninety-five year's old, and he was an alcoholic and smoker. The only thing he did all day was drink and smoke. That was something Tom's parents had been doing all during their retirement. Unlike Tom, they had never had to experience a lack of money. They had a maid to "help" them, so they could sit around all day and do nothing. Their excuse was that they were "sick" and needed help. When Tom called them, they would always create dilemmas in his family life. As a result, Tom continued to get drunk and break things all over the house and hit Nancy.

He would yell at her, "You bitch! You are so lazy! You know how to make me do things for you, but you'll see what I have prepared for you!"

Nancy had to take a lot of abuse because of Tom's parents. This was payback because they had never accepted the fact that Nancy was Tom's wife, and they had to accept her in their lives. Being so far away from them was not doing what it was supposed to do. They were acting like self-centered, old, cranky people who would never realize what life was all about.

Several days had passed since Tom had left when Nancy started to get phone calls from the bank. They wanted to know when Nancy and Tom would be able to make a payment on their business loan. Nancy did not know much about the business affairs, because Tom had been handling everything. The bank kept calling and calling, and Nancy decided to call Tom.

"Please, Tom," she pleaded, "tell me what to do. The bank keeps calling, and they want to know when we'll be able to make a payment."

"Don't worry," Tom told her, "everything is under control. I know you can handle this."

Nancy was going out of her mind. On top of the financial problems, she was also having sinus problems. She had been having them for years, and she had to hold her warm sand pack over her forehead while she dealt with all this craziness. But at least when the banker called again, she was able to give him the information he was so desperate to have. The day was almost over, but Nancy felt like it was going to last forever. It was so expensive to make calls to Europe, and she did not want to bother Tom. One more day was over, and things were looking a little better, at least for a while.

The next day Tom called to see if there were still any problems. For the meantime, everything was quiet. Nancy still felt under pressure, because she was not sure what was going to come up next. Tom was spending time with his father and working on replacing the missing documents, the documents that his half sister may have stolen. She was the only one who visited her father when Tom was not around. She would manipulate him to get what she wanted from him. She was not concerned about him being alone or needing help to cope with his daily needs, only about the money he had and the apartment he lived in.

Tom was disappointed and troubled by the situation. He had to endure his father's heavy drinking problem and out of control spending habits. It was hard for him to explain that eating out at restaurants cost money. His father was a well-known customer at all the neighborhood taverns, with his usual complaining about the meals they served him. Tom's mother had been an excellent cook, and Tom's dad was very picky about how his food was prepared. She had always made such tasty dishes. Her cooking was not to be matched, and Larry was having a hard time accepting other people's cooking. He had loved her pork chops with mashed potatoes and special sauce. When Nancy called, Tom would tell her how he was preparing meals for Larry, and how he never liked his cooking. He was so disappointed.

"Today, I went to the store and bought the best pork chops to cook for my father, but he told me that the meat was burnt and that I wanted to poison him!" he told her.

"Don't worry, Tom," Nancy consoled him, "it's his age talking; it's not your cooking. I know you're an excellent cook and that your meals always taste great. Don't let this get to you."

It was nice to be reassured that his cooking was not the problem, but there was nothing he could do about his stubborn father. Tom was so sick of the smell of cigarettes he had to endure. There was not a room without this smell. He hated the fact that he had to sleep in a room that had the stench of stale cigarette smoke. The windows were yellow, and all of the curtains were missing. There was no a trace left of the once beautifully furnished home he had known. It was a sad picture. Tom was counting the days until the end of his visit. He was fed up, but there was something that needed to be straightened out before he returned home. Finding the missing documents was so much work. He had to go through so much red tape at so many institutions. It was a complicated and time consuming process.

Back at home, Nancy was barely able to keep up with the payments. It was a living hell for everybody. Still, she held on, because she had no choice but to have faith. The days seemed to get longer and longer, because the business was not doing well. There were not enough costumers willing to spend money.

Finally the day of Tom's departure came. Although the day he had left, they had not had very warm relations, Nancy was ready to meet him. It was early in the morning when the plane arrived, and Nancy was at the airport waiting for him. The airport was noisy and full of people. Everyone was anxious to see their loved ones or friends. The flight was on time, and Nancy was at the baggage claim area. There was a warm hug and kiss like nothing had happened, and they did not argue. They took the elevator to the fifth floor and headed to the spot where the car was parked. The weather outside was cold and foggy. There wasn't much traffic because everyone was at work already.

"How was the flight?" Nancy asked. "Did you have breakfast on the airplane?"

"It was a great flight," Tom replied. "I had a nice breakfast, and right now, the only thing I need is a hot bath and a bed."

"I think we can arrange that," Nancy said. "Tell me, how is everybody doing back home?"

"Everyone is fine except for my dad's drinking. But I can't do anything about that. He doesn't want to listen to anybody."

"I am so sorry to hear that," Nancy told him. "I do feel that you are right about not being able to make him stop drinking. As far as I recall, we have been having the same problem with you. I was never able to make you stop either. I don't see any solution to the problem, because I don't think that anyone can help him if he's not willing to listen."

When they got home, Tom was able to take a hot shower and finally get to bed. He decided to stay home and spend the whole day with the family. Jen was home waiting for her boss to call her.

She was in the process of relocating her business, so she told Jen that she was going to call her when she was ready to have her come back to work. It was a good, warm feeling having the whole family together and forgetting about the obstacles for a moment.

The next day, Tom was back to his business responsibilities and Nancy was dealing with the bank that had financed their house. Nancy was so disappointed with the way they treated them and their unwillingness to help. The way the bankers were treating desperate homeowners who were trying to seek help was despicable. Instead of helping, they were giving them the ride of their life. A little while earlier, these same bankers had been so helpful and friendly to these same homeowners because they wanted their business. When the time came to thank them, things got different.

Nancy was busy trying to save the home for which they had worked for so many years. The money for everything was coming from the business. Nancy was dealing with rejection from so many places as she filled out applications for employment, hoping to find extra income and make life easier for the whole family. It was a very tight job market. So many businesses had gone under. People were suffering, and things were not looking so good for the future.

Tom was focusing on advertising. Before the recession, he did not have to do any advertising; but now it was impossible to survive without it. Nancy was helping by making flyers and visiting old friends who had small stores around the area where the business was located.

She told Tom, "What would you do if I didn't have all my friends to help us in these hard times?"

Tom jokingly replied, "What are women for if they can't find a way out of everything? I feel lucky to have you as my best friend and partner in life!"

The times were challenging. Obstacles kept coming at them like huge waves. It was impossible to keep up with even the essential bills, so Tom had to stop paying on his credit cards. Some of their creditors were trying to get higher payments, and this was the end of the road. Nancy was going out of her mind from talking to bankers. One of the banks was hiding behind a collection agency, which was refusing to disclose the name of the bank they were representing. They were coming up with excuses to keep the payments high. Tom and Nancy were running out of money from making huge interest payments, but nobody was acknowledging how hard it was to cope in the tough economy.

At the same time, the biggest banks were playing the victim and collecting money from the government, which was slowly disappearing into executives' pockets. There was no shame or blame involved into the process. Hardworking people were being thrown onto the streets as their houses were taken away. The people were being robbed of their dream and instead given a nightmare. There was no one at the other end of the tunnel to hear their pleas for help. There were so many programs available, but none of the banks were obligated to help. Nancy was disappointed about some of the institutions that had been established to stand up for the people. Instead, they were doing the opposite.

"I think we still can count on the government to protect our rights when we feel they are being violated," she told Tom. "These are very strict people, and I have faith in them."

Tom was tired of all of the troubles surrounding him. It was hard for him to believe that the government was still guarding the best interests of the people. He would tell Nancy, "I think money is the power behind everything, and who are we to expect to be defended? It's hard for me to keep my hopes up."

To this, Nancy would tell him, "I think you are being too pessimistic, and you should look at things differently. Being negative doesn't do any good. We should continue to do what we feel is right and wait for the results."

Time was going by fast, and Nancy was getting close to working out more beneficial terms for one of the loans. After one year, she was finally able to achieve the result she had been praying for. One of the banks gave them a loan modification with the best possible terms, and everyone at home was in disbelief. The impossible terms of the other loan, to everyone's surprise, were strictly upheld by the court, which based its decision on the bank's false allegations and nonsense. It was a typical case of big banks not having any shame and using their power to buy their way out. When they received the letter, Nancy could not hold in her anger. "I just want to write 'Bullshit!' on the letter and send it back to them," she told Tom.

Tom said, "I don't think you're going to gain anything from that. It's better to forget about it."

Nancy was unhappy with the outcome, but she tried to forgive and forget. Tom was preparing to file for bankruptcy, like millions of citizens who were tired of being harassed by the banks. The banks were not losing anything because they had already gotten their money back from the high interest they had been charging people for years and years.

IX

It was not such a hot summer in Denver that year, and many people were losing their homes. There were many new and improved modification programs available, but the problem was the lack of jobs. The real estate market was at an all-time low, and rates were falling, and so were house values. Nancy and Tom were in the worst period of their life together. Business was going from low to nonexistent. The bills were still coming and piling up, and everyone was on the alert. There was no room for hesitation any longer; it was time to switch to survival mode. Making excuses was not an option, and they had to do something quick.

"I don't know how much worse things can get," Tom told Nancy. "I feel like I'm going to have a heart attack. There's no other option available for now. I'll have to look for a job somewhere else."

Nancy said, "I think we should find the most realistic way out of this situation. I don't think having a heart attack will do anything for anybody. Waving a white flag is not a healthy way out."

"You're right," Tom said, "giving up is not a solution. It was just a moment of weakness of my part."

Nancy was happy to hear the answer she needed so badly. It was a very serious situation, and the pressure was overwhelming. There were so many unpaid bills lying around, and this was not making things easier for anyone. Jen was working two jobs just to pay her bills, and it was too much for her to handle. She was beautiful, twenty-year-old girl, full of life, but she was always tired because of work. She wanted to go to school, but the economic situation made that impossible. All of the money was gone, and the family had never had a savings account, because Tom had always taken care of the finances.

Things could have been different, but when Tom's mother was alive, he was sending her all of the money that should have gone into their savings. As long as Jen was alive, she had always had a maid, for which Tom's family was paying without Nancy's knowledge or approval. Tom kept Nancy out of the business, in accordance with Tom's mother's wishes. Tom played the victim caught between two women. He would complain to his mother that Nancy and Jen were spending all of "his" money on clothes and coffee. At home, Tom would tell Nancy that he was "saving" the money he was sending to his mother for her maid services and her life of luxury. His family lived to have the best food and drinks on the table.

Tom and Nancy were the slaves, and his mother and father were the king and queen. They had never helped their son with a penny, but he made sure they never felt robbed of the best that life had to offer. He had to do whatever they felt was right and be quiet. They always ignored the fact that their son was a late-stage alcoholic who existed solely because Nancy was just naïve enough to keep him in her life and worry about what would happen to him if she ever decided to leave him. All of the problems and obstacles the family was facing were a result of Tom's parents. They had never allowed him to love his wife and daughter. They had arranged it so that were the only ones in his life that he was allowed to love. Selfishness was deeply rooted in these people. They were so blinded that they could not see what their selfishness was doing to their son. Tom was too selfish to see that he was not the only one working, but his wife was as well. He never gave his wife credit for anything she did to benefit their family.

Nancy was a devoted wife and mother who never had time to ask herself the most important questions: What do I want to do with my life? Am I happy with Tom? Do I want my life to end like this, serving everybody around me and not doing anything for myself? Nancy was kindhearted woman, and she was always sacrificing her needs to help others. For her, the most important thing was to have a happy family and do her best to provide the best life she could for everyone. On top of working, she did the grocery shopping and everything around the house. Tom was interested in money and nothing else. He was so lazy about doing his chores around the house, and he was giving Nancy added stress because of it.

Life was a full of pressure for Nancy because Tom was an alcoholic and a stubborn man who thought he was always right. He blamed her for all of his failures in life. He was constantly attacking her, but she was always nice enough to ignore it and pretend that nothing had happened. Tom's explosions came so often, and it was hard for Jen as well. Sometimes she had to deal with him. He had no control over his emotions when was drunk. It was impossible to explain to him that the alcohol would not solve their problems and would not make a difference in anybody's life. He was living in denial, just like every person who has had an addiction problem. The only way out was for him to admit to himself that he had a problem.

Nancy would tell him, "You know, Tom, you are not twenty years old anymore, and every organ in your body is being damaged more by drinking than when you were young. If you continue drinking like this, one day, you will collapse and never wake up. Do you want this to happen to you? I do not think so, because then you are not going to be able to experience the great things life has to offer. After all, life is not so bad, if we constantly are not poisoning it."

Tom would answer, "I wouldn't be drinking that much if I did not have so many problems and you were not always making me upset. Drinking less would not be a problem if I did not have so many obstacles."

That summer was strange. One day was cold and the next very cold. It was very confusing for everything – the plants and the people. Nothing was growing the way it should have been. Nancy grew tomatoes every year, but that year her tomato plants did not grow tomatoes. The flowers were blooming and then drying up and falling to the ground instead of producing small, green tomatoes. The rest of the garden was mint and garlic, and neither of these plants had a hard time growing. Nancy was relieved that at least some of the plants were doing fine. She was happy to see her garden every day after work. It was a sanctuary from the crazy world she had to deal with on a daily basis.

It was a harsh summer, and the economy was getting worse. People did not want to spend any money on any items that were not necessities. Everyone was having trouble just meeting their basic needs. The unemployment rate was rising at an alarming rate, and many people were on their way to losing their homes. Nancy was deeply saddened and worried about the trouble their business was in. It was hard for her to cope with everything, and her relationship with Tom was deteriorating every day. She was getting more upset about everything Tom had done in the past, and it was hard for her to forgive. They were spending less time together, and the situation was awkward. They were growing apart every day. Tom wanted so badly to have his freedom. Nancy was hurt and upset because she was fed up with his lies and manipulations, which had gotten them into the situation of not having a penny saved to fall back on. Tom would try to make her feel guilty about the situation.

"Don't try to follow every step I take, and mind your own business," he would tell her. "I am not a liar, and don't try to make me out to be one."

"If I had done half the things you have done to our family," Nancy told him, "you would be in an institution by now. The money you have been stealing and sending to Mommy and Daddy all these years could have helped us live a different life, even in this situation. In case you have not noticed, we are the ones suffering the consequences of your irresponsible actions. What can you say about it?"

"You see what you are doing to me now?" Tom would reply. "You are making me want to jump into my car and never come back. As always, you are being such a bitch, and I can't stand you."

Nancy felt so hurt and helpless in these situations because it was impossible for her to make any needed changes. There was no easy way out of this marriage because of the economic situation and the trouble with the house payments. Furthermore, Nancy knew that this was not the right time to take drastic measures to secure her happiness. She was feeling trapped and humiliated. To make things worse, Tom was making friends with people who did not like Nancy and Jen. There was a lot of jealousy between Nancy and Tom, and everybody was waiting for things to get worse. He was too blind and foolish to figure that out. The only important thing to him was to manipulate and take all of the money he was able to get his hands on. He had been doing that for a long time, and he could not imagine not doing it. He was acting like an enemy of the family. Nancy was in agony, and Jen could do nothing but watch her mother suffer. She had her own life and problems.

It was almost the end of the summer, and it was getting difficult to cope with the situation. Nancy was doing her best, but it was not enough to make things go well for the business. Tom was walking around like a zombie, feeling sorry for himself because he was the one in charge of the family's well-being. The problems were coming one after another, and it was becoming extremely hard to pay the bills.

One day Nancy told Tom, "I don't know how long we can continue like this. There is no way for us to keep the business if things keep going the way they are."

"I don't know what to tell you, Nancy," Tom said, "but things don't look good. We are not going to make it this winter for sure. We must find something else to do; otherwise, we could end up on the street."

It was so stressful for everyone. Nancy was getting scared. The situation was dire. A huge lump was stuck in their throats, and neither of them knew how to swallow it. It was sad because everything was tumbling down. Working hard was not going to solve their problems. Things were more serious than that. Tom was also trying to deal with the situation, but he was reaching for the bottle again and closing into himself. It was a sad household. Everyone was suffering in their own way. Tom was spending a lot of time alone in the den. Nancy was very sad because of it, and she was often crying. It was so hard for her to handle his ignorance. She loved him a lot, but he was not showing any sensitivity. Tom's time was spent behind the computer. It was not a secret that he did not want to have anything to do with Nancy. He would not even want to watch a movie with her after dinner. This was something they had always done before. They loved to sit in front of the TV and watch a good movie. This was no longer a diversion for them.

One day Nancy received news that her uncle was dying. She felt like a prisoner because she did not have money to buy a ticket to be by her cousin's side. She had to deal with the fact that she had not seen her relatives for so long. On the other hand, Tom had the privilege of seeing his relatives more often. He did not feel guilty at all, because his selfishness made him blind and insensitive. The only thing that mattered to him was that there was food on the table and alcohol. His father was being very well taken care of, and he did not have to worry about him not being able to buy food or pay his bills.

Meanwhile, Nancy's mother and brother were suffering from lack of food because her mother's income was not enough. Her brother was unemployed because of the global recession, and Nancy was not into a position to help them. She used to send a little money to them before, but now it was impossible because every penny was important. They were struggling with the business. People were concerned about putting food on the table and keeping a roof over their heads. All of these obstacles were taking a toll on Nancy physically and emotionally.

Nancy told Tom, "If things continue the way they are right now, I'll probably end up in an insane asylum. Sometimes I feel that I can't breathe because the luggage I have to carry is too heavy. I'm sick and tired of worrying about whether or not we'll be able to afford our home and our basic needs."

Tom said, "We have to be strong, Nancy, and try to do our best in order to pay our bills. I know it's hard, but we aren't the only ones in this situation. There are a lot of people like us, and we should continue hoping for the best."

Tom and Nancy were running out of money. The sales they were making were covering the late bills – because they were always behind. Instead of using the money from the profits to buy things to help grow the business, they had to use it to cover their losses. Jen was paying her bills, but she was not able to cover everything. Tom and Nancy had to help her pay some of her bills.

They did not have anybody to help them. The only person who was living close to them was Nancy's father, and he was busy taking care of his own life and family. The last thing they could have expected from him was help. Nancy's stepsister was having the time of her life. She was just finishing her degree at a prestigious university. Money was the last thing on her mind because she had their father around. He was making good money still in his construction company. She had all the privileges and all of his love. Nancy asked for help, but he turned his back on her. He had to ask his wife for permission, but she told him NO. It was a pleasure for her to hear that Nancy's family was having financial problems. It was a painful experience. Although she had known the outcome, she had still been hoping he might help her.

She told Tom, "Desperate people take desperate measures. I was hoping that my dad would help me because I have never asked him for anything in my life. This was one of the most hurtful experiences I've ever had. At this point, there is no turning back. That was it. I don't want to ever see him or talk to him again. My door is closed to him forever."

Tom said, "I think you're overreacting because you are very hurt. If your father called you and asked for help, would you refuse to help?"

Nancy answered, "I don't think that that is going to happen. When I scratch somebody from my life, I do it because I know it's the end. I give people so many chances, like I gave my dad; but he never showed me what I wanted to see in our relationship. There is no way I'm ever going to want him back in my life. This time I will prove it to you."

It was not easy for Nancy to have this conversation with Tom, because her father had betrayed her so many times. She would have liked to give Tom the same treatment as well, but she could not commit to that. There were so many things that kept her from being able to cut her ties with Tom. The most important of which were Jen, the business, and the house.

Winter was almost here, and the weather was getting colder. The rain was coming back, and the leaves were turning yellow. Nancy was getting lonelier because her relationship with Tom was not improving. He was extremely disrespectful and did not allow her to express her opinion about anything. His treatment of her was getting intolerable, and Nancy did not know how to deal with it. She felt trapped. She desperately needed to have friends to help her sort things out, but there were not many around her because Tom was so controlling and never allowed her to have friends.

Then one day a long lost friend called and invited her to have lunch. Her name was Sally, and she was very intelligent and loved Nancy because she was loyal friend. "Hi, my dear Nancy," Sally said cheerfully, "you have no idea how happy I am to hear your voice. Oh, it has been so long since the last time we talked."

"I am happy to hear yours too," Nancy said, "because right now what I need the most is a friend. Things have not been going the way I wanted them to. Financially, it has been torture for a long time. I am having a relationship crisis … and I don't know where to begin."

"Believe me," Sally said, "it has been the same story with me. I'm pregnant, and you know from whom. Financially, my situation is worse than yours. I can't even afford a decent apartment. My boyfriend is not in the best situation either, because as you know, he has two children from his previous marriage. His business is hardly making any money, and he has to work at other places to pay his business expenses. A lot of people I know are in a similar situation."

Nancy said, "Congratulations on your pregnancy. I can't wait to see you. It looks like we have so many things to talk about."

Nancy felt so rejuvenated. She really needed to have a friend with whom she could share all of her troubles and hear theirs.

X

It was a sunny day in September, and Sally called as she had promised to have lunch with Nancy. Nancy was getting ready to go and meet with her. Tom knew about Nancy's plans and had nothing against it. He had known Sally for a long time as well, because she used to come to their house for dinner and used to take care of the family pets when they were on vacation. Sally was a good person, very outgoing and honest. Everything about her was great, and they felt comfortable around her.

"So, you are going to meet Sally today and spend the whole day with her?" Tom asked Nancy.

"Yes," Nancy answered. "I'm so excited because this will be a day away from my duties, and every woman should have the opportunity to spend time with a girlfriend. We haven't seen each other for years, and we have a lot to talk about. She told me that she and her boyfriend are going to have a baby."

Tom said, "Oh, I don't have any doubt about it. It's going to be a lot of fun for both of you. Have a great time, and I'll see you when you come back."

"Bye, Tom!" Dorothy said.

"Bye!"

It was almost noon, and Nancy was driving in her car. It was a beautiful day. She was enjoying the sun. Sally was waiting for her at the restaurant. She was sitting at a table outside. There was an umbrella over the table to give them shade. The restaurant was full of people who were enjoying scrumptious meals. Nancy and Sally had a lot to talk about. It had been five years since the last time they had spoken. Sally was a tall, slender, beautiful, thirty-year-old woman. She had a sunny face, and her smile was always on her face. Although she was six months into her pregnancy, she did not look big. It would have been hard to tell that she was pregnant if not for her belly. When she saw Nancy, she jumped up and gave her a long, warm hug. They were so happy to see each other.

Hi, my dearest Nancy," Sally said. "You look fabulous. You have not aged at all."

"Thank you, my dear, but I know I have aged, because I have a mirror at home; but you look the same to me. The only difference I see is your belly. So many people would kill to have your body when they are pregnant. You haven't gained a pound. You are the same skinny woman I have always known."

"Thank you, but I feel so fat and heavy," Sally said. "I've gained twenty pounds. I feel like a bear, and it's difficult for me to move or sleep."

Nancy told her, "I know being pregnant is not fun, but it's not forever. Soon you'll have a beautiful baby. By the way, do you know your baby's gender?"

Sally told her, "It's going to be a girl, and I'm so happy because I wanted a girl. I can't wait to meet her!"

Nancy said, "I know the feeling, because I wanted a baby girl before Jen was born. I had no idea she was going to be a girl, because there was no way to know back then. When I was told I'd had a girl, I was so excited. At least now you'll be able to pick the colors for your baby. This was something I was not able to do, and I had to buy two of everything."

"Yes," Sally said, "I already have everything ready in pink, so I don't have to spend more than I have to."

It was a wonderful day, and the sun was shining. Nancy and Sally were having a good time talking about a lot of things that had happened since the last time they had seen each other. Sally was telling Nancy about her life and the problems her ex-boyfriend had caused her. As a result of all the drama, she had been forced to hide for a year. It had given her the opportunity to go and visit her parents. But the visit it was not so good, because she could only stay with them for a short time. She was afraid that her boyfriend would find out that she was at her parents' house. She did not want them to have to get involved in her troubles.

It had all started one night when Jen's mother invited some old friends for dinner, and they got to visit with Sally for the first time in many years. They asked her if she would not mind if they introduced her to their son, Harry. Sally's parents' home was a small, one-level house. Her parents were sitting in the dining room, having dinner with their old friends and talking about their children. Their son was a very successful pediatrician who was living in Italy. He was a very busy man and never had time to date. They were worried that he would never get married, so Sally was like a dream come true for them. Sally's family had known these people all their life, and they had known Sally from the time she was a little girl. The plan was to invite their son to visit them for a week, so Sally could meet him and they could see if they liked each other.

The next day, Harry's mother called and told Sally's mother that their son was coming for a visit, and that he would be delighted to meet Sally. Everything was working according to plan. Harry came home as he had promised his parents, and they invited Sally for dinner. Harry was a nice, tall, well built, thirty-five-year-old bachelor. When he met Sally, he felt the chemistry between them right away, and it was not long before he proposed to her. Sally accepted his proposal because she felt for him as well. Harry decided to invite his new fiancée to live with him at his house in Italy, so they could have time to get to know each other better and plan the wedding there. Sally told Nancy that he had the most incredible house by the sea. He even bought Sally a new luxury car and added her name to his bank account. He treated her like a queen. He allowed her to do as much shopping as she liked and to do anything she wanted, but Sally never felt happy.

When Harry invited his parents for a celebration before their wedding, they were disappointed to learn that Sally did not feel that Harry was the man with whom she wanted to spend the rest of her life. Sally apologized to them and packed her things and went back to her boyfriend from the past. She had realized that, even though he was not perfect and they had their differences, she loved him and he was the one with whom she wanted to spend the rest of her life.

Nancy could not believe what Sally was telling her. Her life experience was revolving around a man who was never a gentleman and for whom money had always been a problem. Having the chance to find a smart, intelligent, and handsome man like Harry and not considering him a good match was a huge mistake. She told Sally about her troubles with Tom and his constant abuse. The boyfriend Sally was about to call her baby's father was not much different from Tom in the way he treated women. It was a huge mistake, which sooner or later, Sally was going to realize and regret. Nancy's story made her think about what the future might bring, but for now she was satisfied with how things were going in her life.

Sally was preoccupied with the love she had for the father of her unborn child. Nothing was more important to her than her boyfriend and her baby. Sally told Nancy that if things turned for the worse, she would always have the option to leave him. Further, she had no intention of marrying him. After their visit, Sally and Nancy gave each other a hug and promised to get together again soon, before the baby was born. Nancy felt so happy because of the time she had spent with Sally. She had a shoulder to cry on and someone with whom to share all of her troubles. This was exactly what she needed so desperately.

XI

It was a nice fall day in October, and Nancy was getting ready to go to work. The weather was still sunny and warm, and the trees looked so beautiful with their yellow and brown leaves. People were getting ready for the cold days. The economic situation was still not good, and many people were still losing their houses. It was sad and disturbing because this was not the right time for anybody to suffer. Losing their homes and jobs before Thanksgiving and Christmas was a devastating experience for anyone. So many businesses were closing their doors forever. It was almost impossible to find a job because the demand for jobs was more than what the job marker had to offer. One good thing was that Jen had a job. She was only making minimum wage, so Nancy and Tom were still helping so she would not have to worry about rent and food.

They were still coping with the devastating situation, but the obstacles surrounding them were more that they were able to endure. Their business was not good, but somehow they were still able to pay their bills. There was a time when they had to postpone some of their expenses. Life was like a rollercoaster for them, but they were trying their best. Nancy was trying to find ways to market the business, and she had been able to produce some much needed traffic. People were happy with the services they were providing, and this was helping them gain more customers. The most painful and difficult problem to solve was their constant fights. There was always something that was not right in Tom's eyes, and Nancy was always the one to blame.

Tom's father was still an obstacle. Tom wanted him to be taken care of in a retirement home, but his father did not want to hear about it. He still wanted Tom to leave his family and go back to Poland to take care of him. He did not care about the fact that Tom had so many things in life to deal with. All of this was like yeast for the already bad situation they were in. Most of their arguments were triggered by the helplessness that Tom felt because he did not know what to do to fix this problem. Nancy was the closest one to him, and he was dumping all his frustrations on her. The baggage was too heavy for her to carry. They were like two bombs ready to explode every time they saw each other. Nancy was so upset at Tom's parents that she did not have any desire to know anything about what was going on with them. Nancy and Tom's communication was bad, and this led to their impossible relationship. Tom was living his life, and Nancy had her problems and life as well.

The mastermind of the whole problem was no longer living, but she had left a lasting imprint. Tom and Nancy's relationship was based on the fact that they had known each other since they were teenagers. Neither of them was ready to go and look for someone else. It was a sad and disturbing fact that neither of them was responsible for the situation they were in. Their marriage was broken, and happiness was not a possibility.

XII

It was a rainy day of November, and the sky was cloudy and unfriendly. The birds were sitting on the wet, cold tree branches. The smell in the air was of smoke. Nancy was sitting in her living room looking out the window. Her expression was sad and helpless because she did not know what the future was going to bring. She knew for sure that happiness was something she could only have in her dreams. Love was long gone and never to come back. Now was the time for her to look back in retrospect and start to make plans for the future.

Nancy was brokenhearted about the way her life had turned out. All of her efforts had gone unnoticed. It had all been a waste. She had lived all her life with the hope that one day she would be rewarded for her dedication. She had not wanted diamonds and gold. The only thing she had ever wanted was to have a stable family and a loving husband for the rest of her life. It was the most horrible feeling someone could experience after so many years of effort to be the best wife she could be. She felt used up and left to suffer. Nancy had lost everything at once: the money she had worked so hard for, being next to her husband, and the love she had imagined having with him.

She made the decision to start to think of herself for once. Now was the time to make important decisions and move on with her life. There was not much time left to grieve. The time to make things better was now. She was a middle-aged woman who had to learn to live and build a life around her. This was the only way Nancy could experience the good things life had to offer. The future was in her hands, and she had to act in order to be happy again. Moving forward in life was the best thing to do. Nancy decided not to wait a minute and to start to do something on her own. The good thing was that she had her brother and mother for support – she was not alone. They loved her unconditionally and were there whenever she needed them the most.

She had Jen too, but Jen had her own life and problems to worry about. The troubles she had had to face alongside her mother had impacted Jen as well. She was on the same page as Nancy, because she did not know how to get to where she wanted to go. Tom and Nancy had always been so busy trying to figure out how to solve their own problems that they had never had time to give Jen the support she had needed to help her achieve her goals. Jen had been the adult in the house while they were constantly arguing. She had not been able to be the child she had deserved to be, and this had done its damage. She had been robbed of a normal, peaceful childhood. She was afraid to even think about leaving them alone because she feared what the outcome might be due to their constant fights. She did not want anybody to be hurt, because she loved both of her parents. No child deserved the punishment of living and growing up in the kind of family she had, but this had been Jen's plight. She had endured it her whole life. Things would have been better for her if her father had not been the kind of person he was.

For both Nancy and Jen, it was time to start living for themselves. It was time to try to find a way to make their lives better. Happiness did not seem so elusive now that the constant arguing and fighting had ended. It had taken Nancy's leaving Tom. She had to make the decision to live on her own. It had turned out that the only solution was for Nancy and Tom to dissolve their marriage and live their lives apart for the first time since they were teenagers.

CPSIA information can be obtained
at www.ICGtesting.com
Printed in the USA
FSOW04n0735280515
7471FS